A WOODLAND MYSTERY™

The Secret of the Song

A WOODLAND MYSTERY
By Irene Schultz

The
Wright
Group®

To Carolyn Goetz, who led the fight that saved
the Lake Bluff Wetlands

The Secret of the Song
©1996 Wright Group Publishing, Inc.
©1996 Story by Irene Schultz
Cover and cameo illustrations by Taylor Bruce
Interior illustrations by Meredith Yasui, Tom Boatman, and
Charles Solway
Map illustration by Dave Cap

Woodland Mysteries™
©1996 Wright Group Publishing, Inc.

The Woodland Mysteries were created by the
Wright Group development team.

The Wright Group
19201 120th Avenue NE
Bothell, WA 98011

Printed in the United States of America

10 9 8 7 6 5 4 3

ISBN: 0-7802-7239-0

What family solves mysteries...has adventures all over the world...and loves oatmeal cookies?

It's the Woodlanders!

Sammy Westburg (10 years old)
His sister Kathy Westburg (13)
His brother Bill Westburg (14)
His best friend Dave Briggs (16)
His best grown-up friend Mrs. Tandy
And Mop, their little dog!

The children all lost their parents, but with Mrs. Tandy have made their own family.

Why are they called the Woodlanders? Because they live in a big house in the Bluff Lake woods. On Woodland Street!

Together they find fun, mystery, and adventure. What are they up to now?

Read on!

Meet the Woodlanders!

Sammy Westburg
Sammy is a ten-year-old wonder! He's big for his fifth-grade class, and big-mouthed, too. He has wild hair and makes awful spider faces. Even so, you can't help liking him.

Bill Westburg
Bill, fourteen, is friendly and strong, and only one inch taller than his brother Sammy. He loves Sammy, but pokes him to make him be quiet! He's in junior high.

Kathy Westburg
Kathy, thirteen, is small, shy, and smart. She wants to be a doctor someday! She loves to be with Dave, and her brothers kid her about it. She's in junior high, too.

Dave Briggs

Dave, sixteen, is tall and blond. He can't walk, so he uses a wheelchair and drives a special car. He likes coaching high-school sports, solving mysteries, and reading. And Kathy!

Mrs. Tandy

Sometimes the kids call her Mrs. T. She's Becky Tandy, their tall, thin, caring friend. She's always ready for a new adventure, and for making cookies!

Mop

Mop is the family's little tan dog. Sometimes they have to leave him behind with friends. But he'd much rather be running after Sammy.

Table of Contents

Chapter 1:
A Trip to the Wetlands

It was a bright, cool Sunday afternoon in Bluff Lake.

The Woodlanders were making their way through the tall grass to the edge of a big pond.

Kathy Westburg, thirteen, was holding a brown paper sack. Something was scratching around inside it.

Her ten-year-old brother Sammy said, "Well, let's get this over with."

He ran over to Kathy and looked in the sack.

Two large turtles looked back at him.

He jumped back and held his nose. "Yuck! They still smell awful!

"Butterfly and Biter are nearly the best pets I ever had, but no one can stand them. Not even me!"

2

Kathy said, "I'm sure going to miss them. I loved the way Biter ate bits of Mop's dog food off the floor."

Mrs. Tandy said, "I like the pretty marks on Butterfly's back."

Fourteen-year-old Bill Westburg said, "But how about that pretty SMELL every time you went past their bowl!"

Sammy said, "That was nothing compared to the pretty smell of WASHING the bowl!

"But even if they are stinky, I feel weird about just dumping them in the pond."

Dave Briggs, the Woodlanders' sixteen-year-old friend, smiled.

He rolled himself over to the edge of the pond in his wheelchair.

He said, "Don't feel bad, Sammy. The Wetlands are a perfect place for them."

Mrs. Tandy said, "For one thing, there

are other turtles here! And possums. And raccoons. And birds. And remember all the frogs we saw here last spring?"

She sat down on a log and looked into the pond.

Kathy said, "Sometimes I can't believe this place is right in the middle of Bluff Lake."

Sammy said, "OK. I guess these two smelly turtles will love it here."

He took the turtles out of the sack.

Dave said, "Get ready. Get set. GO!"

Sammy leaned down to the pond and set them free.

They all watched Butterfly and Biter swim away in the calm, dark water.

But just then a stranger came up behind them.

He shouted, "WHAT ARE YOU KIDS DOING HERE!"

His loud, mean voice made them jump.

They turned to look. Standing there was a sour-faced man in a winter overcoat. His long, thin nose was red from the cold. The rest of his face looked frozen.

The man hadn't noticed Mrs. Tandy because she was still sitting down on the log.

5

But slowly Mrs. Tandy stood up. And she was VERY tall. And she was VERY mad!

She looked straight into the man's eyes. She said, "We have a perfect right to be here! Everyone does!"

Bill took a step closer to the man. He frowned and said, "Mrs. Moss is our neighbor. She owns the Wetlands Farm. She lets the whole town come here, so back off."

The man frowned, too. He backed up a little. He said, "Not for long, she won't ..."

Mrs. Tandy took a step toward him.

He turned around fast and hurried away.

They heard him drive off.

A cloud had covered the sun. The day was turning colder.

Dave said, "Come on, guys. Let's get

in the car and warm up. Then let's go talk to Mrs. Moss. I want to find out who that man is."

But Mrs. Moss wasn't home when they got to her house. A neighbor told them she wouldn't be back until late that night.

So they would have to wait until Monday after school to find out.

Chapter 2:
Where's Mrs. Moss?

"Hey, wake up, everybody!" Sammy yelled.

He was standing in the hall in his shorts.

It was 6:00 Monday morning.

He ran down to Bill and Dave's room.

Their little dog Mop ran with him, barking and jumping. Every once in a while he took a friendly bite at Sammy's toes.

Sammy shouted, "Hey, wake up! Look outside! There was a snowstorm. The radio said there's no school today! We can sleep late!"

Bill opened one eye and groaned. "If you woke us up to tell us we can sleep late, how can we sleep late?"

But he got out of bed. He looked out the window.

He said, "Holy cow! There must be about two feet of snow out there!"

The woods were beautiful. Every branch and bush was frosted with snow.

Dave pulled himself into his wheel-chair.

He said, "This is great! Now we won't have to wait to see Mrs. Moss. We can go over this morning and dig her out of the snow."

Kathy came in with Mrs. Tandy. She said, "The snow plow's going down our street now."

They could hear it banging along.

Bill said, "The first thing we should do is dig out our own driveway."

Dave said, "While you dig, Mrs. Tandy and I can make the beds and fix breakfast."

In half an hour Kathy, Bill, and Sammy had the driveway clear.

After a quick breakfast, they all grabbed some shovels and headed for Mrs. Moss's house.

They began to dig a path from the street to her white picket fence.

Dave tied Mop's leash to his wheelchair.

11

Then, from his chair, he helped shovel the path.

They finally made it to the front door.

Sammy knocked on the door and rang the bell at the same time. He said, "Mrs. Moss! It's us! We dug you out! Hello!"

But there was no answer.

Bill tried. He banged on the door.
"Mrs. Moss! Are you all right?"

No answer.

Kathy tried the doorknob. The door
was locked.

Sammy said, "Do you think something
happened to her? She's ninety years old,
you know."

Dave said, "Let's dig around to the
back porch. Then we can shout at her
bedroom window."

They finally got onto the porch. But
they found something that scared them.
The back door wasn't locked.

Bill, Mrs. Tandy, Kathy, and Sammy
hurried inside.

They searched the house. Mrs. Moss
was gone.

They ran back out to Dave.

Kathy said, "You don't think she could

be in her garage, do you? Maybe she didn't lock the door before she went out yesterday. And maybe she got sick driving home."

Mrs. Tandy said, "It's not like Jean Moss to leave her door un-locked."

Bill said, "We better check the garage anyway. Her car's in it. You can sort of see it through the window."

They began to dig fast. When they got to the garage's side door, they found it was stuck shut.

They took turns trying to pull it open.

Finally Sammy got mad. He took a step back.

He said, "Rotten old thing."

Then he kicked the door hard and yanked the knob.

The door opened!

They rushed inside, crowding around the big old car. They were afraid they would find Mrs. Moss sick on the front seat.

But the front seat was empty.

Then from the back of the car, near the floor, a voice said, "Hello? Who's there? Help me out!"

Mrs. Moss was lying on the car floor under a pile of old blankets! She smiled up at them.

She said, "My, I'm stiff from sleeping here. I'm so glad you came.

"I was afraid I'd have to break the garage window to get out this morning. Lucky for me this garage is heated!"

They pulled the covers off of her and helped her into the house.

Mop came along on his leash, jumping and barking in the snow.

Mrs. Tandy said, "Jean Moss, you scared the life out of us. What in the world were you doing out there?"

Mrs. Moss said, "I got home late last night and went to bed.

"But I couldn't sleep. So I turned on the radio.

"I heard a heavy snowstorm was moving in.

"Then I remembered my new bag of birdseed out in the garage. I didn't want it to get snowed in there.

"So I threw on some clothes and went out to the garage. Can you believe the door stuck on me?"

Sammy said, "Yes, because it stuck on US!"

Dave said, "It was lucky you had blankets in the car."

Mrs. Moss said, "I always keep them there in case my car gets stuck in the snow. I'm ninety, you know. Can't be too careful."

She turned on her stove and put on a pot of water.

She said, "Let's have some hot chocolate and the cookies I made yesterday."

She put cups and plates on the kitchen table. She said, "This is a good time to have a little party. A special going-away party."

Sammy asked, "What do you mean? We aren't going anywhere."

Mrs. Moss said, "I know, you sweet boy, but I'm going away." Her voice shook.

Then, cheerful Jean Moss put her hands up to her face. She began to cry like a baby.

Chapter 3:
Mr. Wimp

They all rushed over to her.

Mrs. Tandy hugged her.

Bill wiped her eyes and sat her down.

Kathy said shyly, "Are you sick, Mrs.

Moss? What's wrong? What do you mean, you're going away? Oh, don't cry."

Dave said, "So maybe THAT'S what the man at the Wetlands was talking about ... he said you wouldn't own the land for long."

Mrs. Moss said, "What man, dear? Oh, you must have met Mr. Whip. He has offered to buy the Wetlands from me.

"It seems that I have to move away from Bluff Lake. My children want me to live near them. In a home for old people."

Mrs. Tandy said, "But why? You've lived here all your life.

"You were born on the Wetlands Farm. All your friends are here. Why do you want to leave?"

Mrs. Moss said, "Oh, I don't. But my children are worried because I live alone.

They are afraid I'll fall and get hurt. And no one would know. And I suppose they're right.

"I'll need some money to get into the old people's home. It might take months to sell this place. But I have a chance to sell the Wetlands Farm right away.

"Besides, even if I stayed here in Bluff Lake, I would have to sell the Wetlands."

Bill asked, "But why?"

Mrs. Moss shook her head sadly. "Because my taxes are due next month. They get higher each year. I don't have enough money to pay them any more."

Kathy said, "Mrs. Moss, this is all wrong. You CAN'T move to an old people's home. It might make your kids feel better, but you would hate it."

Sammy said, "Your kids are nearly seventy years old. If they like the home so much, why don't THEY move into it!"

21

Bill said, "I'll bet we can help you get out of this mess. We want you to stay in Bluff Lake. And we want to keep the Wetlands for the town."

Dave said, "It seems to me—"

A loud knock on the door stopped him.

Mrs. Moss went into the living room. She called, "Who is it?"

A loud voice answered, "It's me, Carl Whip! Open the door. It's cold out here. And I don't have all day!"

She opened it.

In walked the man they had seen at the Wetlands. He said, "Here are the papers for you to sign."

Then he noticed the Woodlanders. He said, "So you show up today, too. Are you always under foot?"

He laughed in a mean-sounding way.

He turned to Mrs. Moss. He said,

"Sign these as soon as you can."

Mrs. Moss said, "I want a few days to think things over. I don't want to sell the Wetlands unless I have to, you know."

Mr. Whip said, "Look, Mrs. Moss, I made you a good offer. You better take it right away, or I might decide not to buy. And then you'll be in trouble."

Sammy frowned. He said, "Look Mr. Wimp ..."

"Whip," said the man. "Whip, not Wimp."

Dave said, "Whatever. Stop trying to scare Mrs. Moss."

Bill said, "Leave the papers. She will look them over."

Mrs. Moss said, "Yes, I will phone you when I'm ready, Mr. Whip."

Mop began sniffing Mr. Whip's leg.

Suddenly Kathy called, "Down, Mop! Don't bite!"

Mr. Whip growled, "BITE! Does that little rat bite? Keep him off of me."

He ran out the front door and closed it, except for a crack.

Then he opened it again and shouted, "You better sign those papers by tomorrow!"

Mop thought he was playing. He ran to the door and barked.

Mr. Whip shouted, "Hey, get away from me, you little monster!"

He slammed the door.

Everyone began to laugh ... even Mrs. Moss.

She said, "I feel a lot better. Do you really think we could save my Wetlands for the town?"

Sammy said, "Well, first things first. Let's go get those cookies. THEN we can talk this over."

Chapter 4:
A Secret Surprise

Mrs. Moss said, "How about a real lunch instead of just cookies? I can make the kind we used to have on the Wetlands Farm."

Kathy said, "Thanks, but we ate breakfast before we came over."

Sammy said, "But that was HOURS ago!"

So Mrs. Moss got out some flour and baking powder and butter and eggs and bacon. She took out apple butter and cornmeal.

She made pancakes and cornbread.

In half an hour, lunch was ready.

Sammy said, "Boy, these are the best pancakes I ever ate! If this is farm food, why did you ever move away?"

Mrs. Moss said, "My children didn't want to be farmers. They moved away. Then my husband died, twenty-five years ago.

"I sold most of the farmland then. That gave me enough money to build this house.

"And I thought I would have enough

extra money to last the rest of my life."

Dave asked, "How much land is left?"

Mrs. Moss said, "Thirty-five acres. Ten of the acres are the Wetlands, too wet to build on. But those are the ones the animals love the most."

Sammy said, "Like Butterfly and Biter! I'll bet they've stunk up the whole place by now!"

Bill asked, "So what does Mr. Whip want the land for?"

Mrs. Moss said, "He wants to build houses on it."

Sammy said, "He's so mean, I bet he builds houses that fall apart. He'd put some right on the wet part so they would sink!"

Kathy said, "What was living on the farm like when you were little, Mrs. Moss?"

Mrs. Moss said, "Well, I'll tell you.

It was hard. My parents and I worked from morning till night.

"I remember when my mother was thirty-five, she looked old and worn-out already.

"Every day we milked the cows at four in the morning.

"We carried the milk to the spring house on the edge of the Wetlands. We set the milk in the cool, running spring water."

Mrs. Tandy said, "I'll bet you even made your own butter then."

Mrs. Moss said, "We made our own everything!

"And we raised almost all our own food. We canned fruits ... made jelly ... plowed our fields ... and took care of our horses.

"We had to carry all our water in buckets from the well to the house ... water for drinking, cooking, and bathing.

"My mother was all bent over from having to carry those heavy buckets."

Sammy said, "Your mom must have hated it!"

Mrs. Moss said, "Oh, no. She loved the farm, even with all the work. She and my father had the land all paid for in a few years.

"But my mom kept working as hard as ever.

"She raised chickens for eggs, and for eating.

"She raised ducks and geese.

"She sold the extra eggs and milk.

"She made patchwork quilts to earn more money.

"'Money for a rainy day,' she used to say.

"She kept it in a big brown jar."

Mrs. Moss stood up. She asked, "Would you like to see my mother's mystery quilt?"

Sammy said, "An old quilt? Some mystery!"

Bill poked him.

Mrs. Moss smiled. "My mother began to make a beautiful quilt one day. It was just one month after my father was killed.

"She used her best scraps of cloth ... velvet and silk and satin.

"She told me she was making a

32

special quilt for me.

"She made me promise that I would always keep it.

"She said it would be my treasure."

Kathy asked, "Did you know how to make quilts?"

Mrs. Moss said, "Yes, I used to help her all the time.   But she wouldn't let me help with this one.

"She said this one was a secret surprise for me.   She worked on it only by candlelight, after I was in bed asleep."

Mrs. Moss led them into her room. She opened a wooden chest.

She took out the quilt and spread it out on her bed.

Everyone just stood and stared, even Sammy.

At last Mrs. Tandy said, "Why, Jean, that's the most beautiful quilt I've ever seen."

Kathy said, "I love the pictures on it. Look at that rainbow... and that log house!"

Mrs. Moss said, "That's our farmhouse. Those trees were growing right where they are on the quilt.

"See, an apple tree and a pear tree. And there's the spring house on the edge of the pond."

Dave said, "Look, there's a pot of gold at each end of the rain bow."

Sammy said, "I thought those were pots of chicken soup."

Bill said, "Look at the Wetlands. And that little turtle! And that duck. And a frog. And that big round gray rock below one end of the rainbow."

Mrs. Moss said, "It's near the pond, too. We used to call it Egg Rock. It was bigger than a stove!"

Sammy said, "I don't remember seeing

it in the Wetlands."

Mrs. Moss said, "It was covered by berry bushes long ago. I haven't seen it in twenty years."

Kathy said, "What does the letter N on the side of the quilt mean?"

Mrs. Moss said, "My mother's name was Nancy."

Mrs. Tandy said, "The other side of the quilt has a bunch of brick-shaped patches. With stitches around every brick. I wonder why?"

Mrs. Moss said, "Those stitches are the quilting. They hold the stuffing layers in place.

"See, this is really two quilts. My mother sewed them together around all the edges, back to back."

Dave said, "Hmm ... that's funny. Why would she make it like that?"

Mrs. Moss said, "Well, my poor mother

started acting strange that last year. She kept saying the quilt had two secrets she would tell me someday."

Sammy said, "Secrets! So THAT'S the mystery!"

Chapter 5:
The Song

Mrs. Moss said, "But I don't know the
secrets. Mother died before she told them
to me. She was only forty-two years old."

Sammy said, "Then you were an

orphan like us."

Mrs. Moss nodded and went on. "All that last year she used to sing a strange song to me."

Kathy said, "What was it? Do you still remember it?"

Mrs. Moss said, "Oh, yes. I remember it well. She sang it to the tune of 'Twinkle, Twinkle, Little Star.' It went like this:

"Milk and eggs the money make
Mix them up to make a steak
Someday Jeanie will give thanks
Riches in the Wetlands banks
Milk and eggs the money make
Mix them up to make a steak."

Sammy said, "Wow, strange is right! You can't make a steak with milk and eggs! Pancakes, MAYBE.

"And there aren't any Wetlands banks, are there?"

Mrs. Moss said, "No, and the only bank around here is the Bluff Lake Bank.

"Mother was really sicker than I knew. One day she couldn't even get out of bed. She called me to her.

"She said it was time I knew the two secrets. She said there was one for each side of the quilt.

"'The quilt will make you rich,' she told me. Then she fell asleep. She never woke up again."

Dave said, "I'm so sorry, Mrs. Moss."

Bill said, "But ... did you ever take the quilt apart?   It sounds like your mom was hiding something inside it for you."

Mrs. Moss said, "Yes.   A few months later I thought of Mother's last words.   I opened the stitches along one side.

"I looked in between them.   There was nothing.   So I sewed them together again."

Kathy asked, "What happened to you after your mom died?"

Mrs. Moss said, "It's funny how life works out.   The family on the farm next to mine wanted to farm my land.

"They were crowded at their place.

"Their grandmother and one daughter came to live with me.

"We took care of each other.   We were like a family.

"I ended up marrying one of the sons. Ted Moss.

"But even with his help I could never figure out the secrets of the quilt."

Dave said, "Mrs. Moss, now we have four mysteries to solve ... how to pay your taxes ... how to save the Wetlands ... and the two secrets of the quilt.

"Let's go home, guys. We have a lot to figure out."

The Woodlanders thanked Mrs. Moss for lunch, and left.

As they went outside, Sammy said, "Look! The snow's beginning to melt by itself! After all our work!"

Dave said, "Well, it's a good thing, because we have to go to town tonight."

Mrs. Tandy said, "What's happening in town, Dave?"

Dave said, "Today's Monday. It's the second Monday of the month, right?"

Sammy said, "So what?"

Dave said, "So the town board meets

tonight, that's what."

Bill said, "And?"

Dave said, "And the five of us can go to the meeting. We can tell the leaders about the Wetlands. And Mr. Whip and Mrs. Moss."

Kathy said, "That's a great idea! People from the newspaper may even be there. They'll tell the whole town about it in the paper tomorrow."

Mrs. Tandy said, "We could also talk about setting aside a greenbelt for Bluff Lake."

Sammy said, "What's a belt got to do with this?"

Bill said, "Not a belt, Sammy. A greenbelt."

Dave said, "It means green land for your town, where no houses can be built."

Kathy said, "Do you guys think our town could buy the Wetlands so Mr. Whip can't get it? Could we somehow get enough money together?"

Dave said, "Maybe, but it would take time. And a lot of people would have to help."

Mrs. Tandy nodded.

Bill said, "Hey! Let's talk to people BEFORE the meeting!"

Kathy said, "We could even start a petition!"

Sammy said, "A pet-ish-un? Now you're talking about pets!"

Bill said, "No, Sammy. A petition is a paper that people sign. It's a way for people to tell their leaders what they want."

Sammy said, "You mean it could say SAVE THE WETLANDS or something?"

Dave said, "Sure it could! Let's go get ready."

They hurried into the house and took off Mop's leash.

They grabbed their school notebooks.

They each made up a sheet that looked like this:

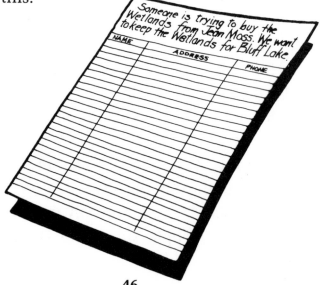

Someone is trying to buy the Wetlands from Jean Moss. We want to keep the Wetlands for Bluff Lake.

NAME	ADDRESS	PHONE

46

Sammy said, "I'll get a million people to sign this!"

Bill laughed. He said, "There are only five thousand people in the whole town."

Dave said, "I'll take my petition to the stores in town. There's less snow there, so my chair will move better."

They went outside.

Dave lifted himself into his hand-controlled car.

Sammy said, "I'll go with you."

He put Dave's chair into the back of the car.

Bill said, "Drop me off at the other end of town, would you?"

Kathy called, "Let's all meet at the train station at five o'clock."

Bill said, "Good idea. Lots of people come home from work around then."

Mrs. Tandy said, "I think most of them will sign."

Sammy said, "Let's get going. Even if I can't get a MILLION people to sign, I bet I'll get the MOST, Bill!"

Bill answered, "We will see about that, my bragging brat-brother!"

And off they drove in the wet snow.

Chapter 6:
The Power of a Cookie

Kathy and Mrs. Tandy went to the houses on Woodland Street.

They split up, then rang doorbells all afternoon.

Some people weren't home.

Some people didn't want to sign.

Some people signed right away.

One man was angry when his bell rang. He told Kathy, "Don't bother me. I'm too busy."

Kathy felt bad. But she went to the next house.

The woman there said she thought it was a great idea.

She got some paper and made a petition page for herself.

She put on her coat and boots and said, "I'll be at that meeting tonight, too."

Mrs. Tandy had a slow time of it.

Half the people who opened the door knew her. They wanted her to come in and visit with them.

Meanwhile, across town, Bill rang one doorbell and got a surprise.

One of his teachers from Bluff Lake Junior High opened the door.

Bill said, "Gosh, Mrs. Cheng. I didn't know you lived here."

When he showed her the petition, she signed right away.

Then she gave him some apple juice and cookies.

Dave had good luck in the hardware store. The owner asked all the people in the whole store to sign.

51

At one house where Sammy stopped, an old man lived alone.

He told Sammy he would sign. But he asked Sammy to shovel the snow off his steps first.

Sammy did, to get him to sign.

At 5:00 they all met at the train station as planned.

Kathy was shaking with cold.

Mrs. Tandy's fingertips were numb.

Bill had fallen on a piece of wet ice. The seat of his pants was soaking wet.

Dave's chair had stuck in the snow. A woman had helped push him out. He was tired. He could hardly make it to the train station.

Sammy ran up last.

He was holding a big paper bag.

His nose was red and runny.

But ... they had over 150 names on

their petitions.

Kathy counted and wrote the numbers down.

Mrs. Tandy 24
Dave 43
Bill 35
Sammy 29
Kathy 32

Sammy said, "See, I told you I'd get the most."

Bill said, "But, Sammy, you don't have the most!"

Sammy said, "I mean by six o'clock I will. Watch this!"

He took two pieces of cardboard out of his bag.

They were tied together by two strings. He said, "I made these at the grocery store." He put them on.

One hung in front of his chest.
The other hung over his back.
There was writing on them. It said

READ
THIS
GET A
FREE
COOKIE

He had cookies in his bag.
People got off the trains. They were
tired and hungry.
When they saw Sammy, they smiled.

They walked over to him.

Most of them signed the petition and ate a cookie.

One man said, "I don't see how we could get enough money to buy the Wet lands from Mrs. Moss."

Sammy said, "We can find a way."

The man said, "Well, if you young ones think so, I'll sign."

Sammy gave him an extra cookie.

By 6:00 they had 310 names.

And Sammy had the most.

He said, "Never forget the power of a cookie!"

Chapter 7:
Mr. Whip Gets Mad

The cold, wet Woodlanders drove home.

They put on dry clothes.

They heated up some home-made soup to go with salad and sandwiches.

After a while Mrs. Tandy said, "I'm beginning to feel like a human again."

Bill said, "Me, too. I felt like a cold dead fish. The soup saved my life."

Dave said, "Don't get too comfortable. It's time to go to the meeting."

Sammy groaned, "Being a hero is hard work! But think how happy those stinky turtles will be if we save their home!"

Everybody laughed, and went to put on their coats.

They drove to the town hall.

They went into the meeting room.

The seven men and women of the town board sat behind a long table.

The Woodlanders sat down.

Janet Jasper was the leader of the town board. She asked if anyone wanted to speak.

Bill stood up. He held their petition papers in his hand.

He said, "I'm Bill Westburg. This is my family."

Janet Jasper said, "Aren't you the Woodland family? Police Chief John Hemster says you've helped him many times."

Bill said, "Yes, we are. We learned this morning that Mrs. Jean Moss might have to sell the Wetlands. That's why we are here."

Then Sammy stood up and said, "We've been out all day with our petitions. We got three hundred and ten names. These people all want the town to save the Wetlands."

Another person said, "That can't be done. Mrs. Moss has said she MUST sell that land for tax reasons. The town planning group has agreed that after the sale, houses can be built there."

Mrs. Tandy stood up. She said, "What

do you mean, CAN'T BE DONE? The planning group can change its mind."

A man said, "I'm Rick Gomez, head of the planning group. And I'm telling you, we won't change our minds."

Dave said, "Mr. Gomez, leaders are picked to serve the people. If we think our leaders are wrong, we have the right to let them know."

Then the woman who made her own petition stood up.

She said, "I think the town is lucky to have the Wetlands.

"They're full of wild life and native plants.

"We should save them for our children.

"Then our children can show the Wetlands to their children."

Janet Jasper said, "You're trying to stand in the way of change."

Kathy couldn't stay quiet any longer.

She stood up.

She said, "Yes. Some change makes things better. But some change makes life worse. Losing the Wetlands makes things worse for Bluff Lake."

Janet Jasper said, "But we can't just tell Mr. Whip we've changed our minds."

Sammy said loudly, "You care more about that rat Mr. Whip than you do about our town?"

Bill poked him.

Sammy stuck out his tongue.

The meeting went on for about an hour.

Everyone had something to say.

Some people had been to the Wetlands. Some hadn't.

By the end of the meeting, the people had decided two things.

They would ask the planning group to tell Mr. Whip to back off for a while.

And the whole town board, all seven, would visit the Wetlands the next week end.

Saturday morning at 10:00 the Woodlanders met the town board members at the Wetlands.

The weather had been dry and warm all week.

The dry grass was a golden color.

The reeds and wild flowers were all dried up. They had turned beautiful brown colors.

There were oak trees in the dry places around the Wetlands. Red-brown leaves still stuck to them.

Janet Jasper said, "It's beautiful here. I had no idea it was like this. I see why you kids want to keep the Wetlands."

Just then a thin, mean-looking man walked up.

It was Carl Whip.

He said, "What are you folks doing here on my property?"

Sammy said, "YOUR property! No way! Did Mrs. Moss sign those papers?"

Mr. Whip said, "No, but she will. She needs the money."

Janet Jasper said, "Mr. Whip, there IS a chance the planning group will change its mind.

"This part of the Wetlands seems far too wet to build on anyway."

Mr. Whip said, "I can have gravel dumped into it. Then I will build."

Mr. Gomez said to Ms. Jasper, "Our planning group DID say he could if Mrs. Moss sells."

Mr. Whip said, "Yes, you did. And if you try to stop me now, I'll sue the town.

"And I'll sue you, Janet Jasper.

"And I'll sue the rest of the town board.

"You'll be sorry if you listen to those brats."

Bill was mad. He saw Mr. Whip was standing right in front of a patch of thorns and sticky burrs.

He shouted, "Watch out, Mr. Whip! Is that a SNAKE near your foot?"

Mr. Whip jumped back.

His skinny legs shook.

He jumped right into the burrs.

"Where?" he shouted. "Where is it?"

Bill said, "Oh, I guess I made a mistake. That snake must've been a stick."

Mr. Whip looked down at his legs.

He said, "Hey! What's poking me?"

Then he saw his pants were covered with burrs.

The board members walked back to their cars, trying not to laugh.

So did the Woodlanders.

Mr. Whip shouted, "You brat! You'll be sorry for this!"

Bill called back, "Well, Mr. Whip, why don't you sue ME, too!"

Then he trotted to the car.

Chapter 8:
The Money Bricks

The Woodlanders drove right over to Mrs. Moss's house. They told her most of the board wanted to help her save the Wetlands for the town.

Mrs. Moss had tears in her eyes. She said, "I can't believe I may not have to leave here! Are you sure about this?"

Sammy said, "Sure we are sure! The only trouble is, it may take a long time."

Bill said, "And we know you need your tax money SOON."

Mrs. Moss said, "I knew it was too good to be true."

But Dave said, "I think we are forgetting something important."

Kathy asked, "What's that?"

Dave said, "The quilt. The two secrets. Mrs. Moss's mother MUST have hidden SOMETHING in there."

Mrs. Moss said, "Well, let's look at it again!"

She led them into her room and took out the quilt.

She said, "Well, I guess I'll try cutting this open one more time. Maybe I missed something all those years ago."

She took a little pair of scissors from a box on her dresser.

The scissors were shaped like a bird with long legs. It was a stork.

She said, "Storks bring good luck. Did you know that? Maybe this stork will help us solve the mysteries!"

The stork's mouth opened and closed as Mrs. Moss cut the stitches.

The brick quilt and the picture quilt came open at the top like a giant bag.

They all looked inside.

They didn't see anything.

Then Dave said, "Try cutting the stitches all the way around. Cut the two quilts apart."

Snip ... snip ... snip ... snip.

They laid the brick quilt down.

They all began looking at the other quilt, the picture quilt.

Kathy felt along its edges.

Sammy said, "The farm looks so real ... I wish all those things were still in the Wetlands where they used to be."

Mrs. Moss said, "Well, part of the chimney of my old house is still there."

Bill said, "Oh, I know where that is. It's a big bunch of field stones. We've made a camp fire there."

Mrs. Tandy said, "I bet I know exactly where the spring house was."

Kathy said, "Me, too. The little spring still runs at the edge of the Wetlands."

They kept turning the picture quilt around and trying to feel something inside of it.

No luck.

Dave said, "We may have to cut it open."

Kathy said, "Let's take a look at the other quilt first."

Sammy picked up the brick quilt. He turned it over. He said, "It just feels like real thin stuffing inside."

Then Bill called, "Wait a minute!"

Sammy said, "What's wrong?"

Bill said, "Look at that corner. There's some stuffing sticking out."

Mrs. Moss said, "I must have cut some quilting threads by mistake."

Bill grabbed the corner. He shouted, "Wow! Check this out!"

He picked up the scissors and cut a few more threads.

He reached into the brick shape at the corner.

He pulled something out.

It was money ... an eighty-year-old ten-dollar bill. It looked fresh and new.

Sammy shouted, "Holy hot dogs! Old money! Look how big it is!"

He did a wild dance around the room. His hair stuck out.

He made his killer-snake face.

He yelled, "I bet there's more!"

Dave said, "I bet there's at least one bill inside every brick shape."

Kathy counted the bricks along one side.

She said, "There are twelve bricks across."

Bill said, "And thirty rows."

Dave said, "That means there may be more than three hundred and sixty bills in this quilt."

Kathy said, "Would that be enough to pay this year's taxes, Mrs. Moss?"

Mrs. Moss said, "I'm afraid not. Not even if they're all ten-dollar bills."

Dave said, "Don't worry, Mrs. Moss. It WILL be enough. Don't you see?

"This money is about eighty years old. Mrs. Moss can sell it to the coin shop for MUCH more than ten dollars a bill."

Mrs. Tandy said, "Jean, give me the stork scissors. I can start cutting while you folks round up some knives."

In a minute they all were cutting stitches on the brick quilt.

One by one they pulled out the bills.

Ten-dollar bills, mostly.

Some twenty-dollar bills.

Some of the bricks had two bills inside.

Soon they had a big pile of cloth and stuffing on the floor.

And they had a big pile of old money in a box on the bed.

Dave said, "Your mother must've turned in her egg and milk money at the bank for new bills. They're perfect, and I think they're worth a lot."

Mrs. Tandy said, "Oh, Jeanie, this is wonderful! Now you can pay your taxes for the year AT LEAST. And take your time to decide about the Wetlands."

Kathy said, "I KNEW we would find a way for you to keep living here.

"And we can find someone to live here with you. Then you can stay here forever."

Mrs. Moss began crying again.

Kathy said, "Oh, no, what's wrong now?"

Mrs. Moss said, "I'm just so happy, it makes me cry. Don't pay any attention to me."

Sammy said, "Gosh, Mrs. Moss. If you cry when you're happy, and you cry when you're sad, you'll be wet all the time!"

Mrs. Moss smiled. "You see, I feel like my mother talked to me today. And now I know her secret after seventy-seven years.

"She got this stake together for me, so long ago. When I was only thirteen! Now she's given it to me all these years later."

Bill shouted, "A STAKE! That must be what the first part of the song means ... 'Milk and eggs the money make. Mix them up to make a STAKE.'"

Sammy said, "Oh, I get it! Not a steak you eat. A STAKE like a bunch of money! She mixed her milk money and her egg money and put it in this quilt!"

Dave said, "This proves something else, too, Mrs. Moss."

She asked, "What's that, dear?"

Dave said, "Since there really was one secret in this quilt, there must be two. The rest of your mother's song must make sense somehow."

Kathy asked, "Don't you think we should open the other side up, too?"

Mrs. Moss said, "Well, my stork scissors were lucky once. I suppose I should try it again. But I hate to cut up the picture quilt."

Mrs. Tandy said, "Why don't you sing the other part of the song again, Jean?"

So Mrs. Moss sang, "Someday Jeanie will give thanks.   Riches in the Wetlands banks ..."

Just then they heard a really loud noise.

Bill said, "That's the Bluff Lake fire whistle!"

Then the phone rang.

Mrs. Moss answered it.

They heard her gasp, "My goodness!"

Chapter 9:
Fire

Mrs. Moss hung up the phone.

She said, "I can't believe it!"

Sammy said, "What's wrong?"

Mrs. Moss said, "That was Police Chief Hemster calling."

Sammy said, "Really? Maybe he was calling for Mrs. Tandy since he's her BOY-friend."

Bill poked him and said, "What happened, Mrs. Moss?"

Mrs. Moss said, "There's a fire over at the Wetlands."

Sammy yelled, "You're kidding! Let's GO!"

Dave wheeled over to grab his coat. He said, "Come on, guys."

Mrs. Moss said, "I'll take my broom to help beat out the fire. Sammy! Kathy! Bill! Get the leaf rakes and old brooms from the garage!"

When they got to the Wetlands road, they all piled out near the hill.

Three fire trucks were parked there, too.

Chief Hemster waved to them. He said, "Am I glad to see you! Just choose your places and start in. Stay away from the fire, but get those flying sparks."

The fire was flaming high on the other side of the hill.

It raced through the thick bushes on one side of the pond.

There was a strong wind blowing. Sparks flew over the hill to the fields.

The Woodlanders grabbed their rakes and brooms.

They ran after the sparks and started beating them out.

Other town people who lived near the Wetlands were beating out sparks, too.

Every few seconds a rabbit or chipmunk ran past them.

A muskrat ran out of the Wetlands, right past Sammy.

Sammy yelled, "Hey! I almost hit it by mistake!"

Kathy moaned, "All the poor birds and animals!"

Bill yelled, "I think the fire fighters have it under control. Look, there's more smoke than fire now!"

Dave said, "Get that spark in back of you, Mrs. Tandy!"

In twenty minutes the fire seemed to be mostly out.

The fire fighters came around the hill.

One of them said, "Thanks, everybody. It's OK now."

The town people who had been help-
ing started for home.

The fire chief said, "We are leaving
two people here. They'll call if it flames
up again."

Bill said, "Is it all right if we stay,
too? We can help look out for new fire."

The fire chief said, "That would be a
big help. But be careful."

Then he added, "It's a shame about
all the wild berries. But we saved the
trees and most of the land."

Mrs. Moss said, "I'm so glad. Those
are sugar maples over there. I used to
get maple syrup from them."

Dave said, "I've been thinking ... it
seems strange for a fire to start in those
bushes."

Bill said, "True. Hardly anyone goes
near them, not even to pick berries in
the summer."

Sammy said, "Who would? Except me, of course. Those thorns are killers!"

The fire chief said, "These fires can be tricky. Sometimes a spark gets into roots under the ground.

"Then a fire can burn for days in there. It can break into flames when you least expect it."

Kathy said, "Come on. Let's start raking the burned-over part. We don't want anything else to burn."

Dave said, "Let the fire fighters do the inside. We can go around the outside edges."

They began to rake.

The fire fighters were knocking down the black, burned branches.

Their big boots and fire coats were covered with wet ashes.

Suddenly Mrs. Moss pointed to where one of them was working, near the edge of the pond.

She whispered, "Look at what the fire gave back to the Wetlands!"

They saw a big, egg-shaped rock. It was black from smoke. It was as big as a stove.

"Hey!" Bill shouted. "It's the rock on your quilt! The one that disappeared! That's Egg Rock!"

Chapter 10:
The Crab Apple

Sammy ran right over the wet, sooty ground up to the big rock.

He tried to hug it, but it was too big.

He dived on top of it ... and slid down the other side.

Kathy called, "Sammy, are you all right?"

He picked himself up.

He had a silly grin on his face.

He was covered with black soot.

He said, "I'm OK. But boy, is that a sneaky rock. You'd have to be part spider to climb it."

Mrs. Moss laughed. "I could never climb it when I was a child, either."

Mrs. Tandy said, "Isn't it great that we can all see it again! I LOVE this place!"

A man came walking up in back of them.

It was Carl Whip.

He said, "Sure, lady, you love it.

"A dirty rock.

"A slimy pond.

"A filthy burned-out acre of thorn-bushes and a bunch of ratty animals."

Sammy came running over.

He stopped right in front of Mr. Whip.

He made his bull-dog face.

He was covered with soot.

His hair stuck out like one big burr.

He began jumping all around.

He shouted, "Mr. Whip, you're so stupid! You don't know anything about nature at all!

"I bet it was YOU who set fire to the bushes, you ... you ... stinky rotten old crab apple!"

For a minute Carl Whip stood staring at Sammy.

His mouth fell open.

Then his crabby face began to wiggle.
And suddenly it changed completely.
The corners of his mouth pulled up.

Carl Whip began laughing so hard he couldn't talk.

He finally said, "Just a minute there. I've been called a lot of things in my life. But this is the first time I've been called a stinky rotten old crab apple.

"And I may look mean.

"And I may talk mean.

"And maybe I don't like kids.

"But I'm NOT a criminal. I don't set fires."

Dave said, "Listen, Mr. Whip. We really need to talk with you."

Mrs. Tandy added, "Let's all go back to our house and let Sammy get cleaned up. It's nearly three o'clock. We could get some food, sit down, and really talk together."

Mrs. Moss said, "My, I'm tired. I could use some sitting down."

Mr. Whip said, "Well, I might as well listen to what you folks have to say."

He pointed to Sammy. "This mud ball over here has quite a mouth on him. He sure got my attention."

Bill said, "I'll ride in your car and show you the way."

So they all drove home.

The Woodlanders made Mrs. Moss and Mr. Whip comfortable in the living room.

Sammy headed straight for the shower.

Dave and Mrs. Tandy brought in a big plate of sandwiches and a huge plate of oatmeal cookies. Mr. Whip started in on the cookies.

Bill and Kathy brought them coffee and milk.

In a few minutes Sammy was back.

He was clean from head to toe.

After eating two sandwiches, he said, "MAN! You should have seen the shower floor. It looked as muddy as the Wetlands."

Bill said, "I DID see it. It was WORSE than the Wetlands pond. It would have killed a turtle!"

Sammy said, "Your NORMAL bath water would kill a turtle. Pass me the cookies."

Dave said, "Mr. Whip, I have an idea. It might help settle our Wetlands problem."

Mr. Whip said, "Well, tell me. After all, even a rotten old crab apple can listen once in a while. So what do you have in mind?"

Dave said, "Mrs. Tandy told us about greenbelts for towns."

Mr. Whip said, "What's that got to do with me?"

Mrs. Tandy said, "Well, the story I read said that sometimes builders GIVE land for greenbelts."

Mr. Whip got his mean look back.

He said, "Well, I'm not about to give away land. I spend good money to get it. I would go broke doing that."

Mrs. Tandy said, "But sometimes builders don't lose money doing it. Sometimes they pay lower taxes, to make up for it. And the town helps the builder, too."

Dave said, "Mr. Whip, I want you to go look at the Wetlands with us."

Mr. Whip said, "I've seen it. Thorns, rats, bees, and weeds. What's your point?"

Sammy said, "It's full of wonderful things!"

Mr. Whip said, "Well, let me have another one of those cookies, and I WILL go take another look."

Sammy grabbed ten cookies.

He pushed them into Mr. Whip's coat pocket.

Mrs. Tandy grabbed the whole plate of cookies, and they all rushed out to the car.

Chapter 11:
Cattails and Bloodroots

They all drove to the hill in the Wetlands.

They went over to the pond, near the part of land that hadn't been burned.

Bill said, "Here's the first wonderful thing."

He broke off a stem.

There was a dry brown pod at the end of it, shaped like a pointed egg.

Bill broke it open. "Look at this, Mr. Whip."

Inside were rows of silky white seeds.

Mr. Whip said, "So what is it?"

Bill said, "It's a milkweed pod."

Dave said, "In a few weeks, the other pods will break open, and the seeds will float out on the wind.

"Each one will start a new milkweed plant next spring. By summer the plant is green ... and has sticky milky stuff in it."

Sammy said, "It's weird! Caterpillars eat the leaves. They LOVE them. Later the caterpillars turn into butterflies. Monarch butterflies."

Mrs. Tandy said, "Every fall thousands of those butterflies get together around the milkweed plants."

Kathy said, "They meet in the Wetlands. They're beautiful, all black and orange, dancing in the air."

Dave said, "And you're not going to believe what happens next.

"Those thousands of butterflies band together with others. Then the Monarchs fly to the south, thousands of miles. They find a warm place for the winter."

Mr. Whip said, "You're kidding me. Come on. Thousands of miles?"

Kathy said, "It's true!"

Sammy ran ahead. "Now come over here! Look at these cattails!"

Bill took out his pocketknife.

He cut a cattail stem.

Sammy grabbed it.

He said, "It looks just like a hot dog

on a stick, doesn't it? But watch!"

Suddenly, he hit it against Bill's back.

The cattail top broke apart. It exploded in a cloud of fluff.

It stuck all over Bill's hair.

Bill ran after Sammy. He grabbed the cattail and hit Sammy over the head with it.

Then he threw it in the pond.

Dave said, "They're great for hitting brothers. And, you can eat them. The roots, that is."

Mrs. Tandy said, "Look there, near your elbow, Mr. Whip. That's a wild plum tree."

98

Sammy said, "Hey, what about the wild berries! And wild onions in the spring!"

Mr. Whip said, "But what about all these dried-up weeds?"

Kathy said, "Mr. Whip, these aren't weeds. Those are wild plants.

"People just call them weeds when they grow in the wrong places.

"Lots of them grow flowers, with wonderful names, too. There's butter-and-eggs. It's two colors of yellow.

"And horsetail. It's a plant family millions of years old.

"And there's shooting star."

Sammy said, "How about bloodroot! It oozes orange blood when you break the stem. And you can spread it on things."

Bill said, "Things like your big brother's shirts, right?"

Dave said, "Last summer Kathy and I counted fifty-six different plants in the Wetlands."

Smiling, Kathy looked at Dave. "And I bet there were some we missed."

Just then the sun went down behind some clouds.

Night was coming.

The clouds turned gray with pink and gold edges.

The sunset was so beautiful, no one wanted to talk.

Then Bill said, "We'd better get back to the car."

Mr. Whip said, "It IS beautiful here ... I think we must be able to figure out SOME way to let Bluff Lake keep the Wetlands."

Sammy ran up to him and took hold of his hand.

He said, "Mr. Whip, you're going to be glad you did this! You're not a crab apple after all.

"I can take you back to the pond next spring.

"We can catch a million tadpoles in a jar. I'll show you how to take care of them while they grow into frogs."

Mr. Whip said, "As long as you don't hit me with a cattail, Sammy, it's a deal!"

Chapter 12:
The Map

The next morning Mr. Whip and Mrs. Moss went to a special meeting with a lawyer.

As it turned out, Mr. Whip would buy

the Wetlands from Mrs. Moss ... but he would build only on the high parts of it.

The town would get the pond and the Wetlands ... and the land where the farm buildings used to be.

Later that day Mr. Whip met with the planning board members.

Mr. Gomez was there. He said, "Mr. Whip, I'm surprised you listened to those kids."

Mr. Whip said, "Those kids care about Bluff Lake. And they got me to care, too. I may even come to Bluff Lake to live."

The Woodlanders met Mrs. Moss at her house.

Mrs. Tandy said to her, "Jean, we've taken care of three problems.

"Now you can pay your taxes and stay in your house.

"And we know at least one secret of

the quilt. And the Wetlands are saved for the town."

Mrs. Moss's eyes started to water.

Sammy said, "Now before you start crying on us again, let's figure out secret number two.

"Let's look at the quilt and find out what your mother meant by the second part of her song, 'Riches in the Wetlands banks.'"

They followed Mrs. Moss to the bed-room.

They looked at the quilt.

Bill said, "Well, there's Egg Rock, just where it really is, near the pond."

Dave moved his wheelchair slowly around the bed to one side of the quilt.

He pointed to the letter at the edge.

He said, "Do you know what? I don't think that letter N stands for Nancy at all."

Kathy said, "Then what do you think it stands for?"

Dave said, "I think it stands for NORTH. I think we are looking at more than just a pretty quilt. I think Mrs. Moss's mother made a map of the Wet-lands."

Mrs. Moss said, "Why would my mother leave me a map?"

Bill said, "I'd leave a map to show

where I buried something ... like a treasure map with an X marking the hiding place."

Sammy said, "But there aren't any X marks on this quilt. Everything on it is a real thing. Except the rainbow. And the pots of chicken soup ... I mean gold."

Bill said, "Sammy, THAT'S IT! If this is a map, the POTS must be the marks!"

Sammy said, "But the song says 'Riches in the Wetlands banks.' So how can it be buried?"

Kathy shouted, "I KNOW!"

They all stared at her. It took something very important to make Kathy shout.

Her face was red. She said, "We are thinking of the wrong kind of banks!"

Bill said, "She's right. One pot must be where the spring house used to be, on the bank of the spring! One pot is near Egg Rock, on the bank of the pond!"

Mrs. Moss said, "Oh, my! This is like some mystery novel!"

Dave said, "Get some shovels, guys. Let's find out how this novel ends!"

Chapter 13:
The Buried Treasure

They phoned Chief Hemster.

In twenty minutes they met him at the Wetlands with the quilt.

Sammy spread out the tools.

They had two spades and a hand shovel from Mrs. Moss's garage.

They had a fork, a pickax, and two more spades from their own garage.

They showed Chief Hemster the quilt and told him Mrs. Moss's story.

The chief said, "You've sure been busy. Why didn't you let me in on the fun sooner?"

Sammy grinned. He said, "We should have. Then you could have been with your GIRLfriend this whole time!"

Mrs. Tandy tried to catch Sammy, but he was too quick for her.

Chief Hemster said, "Well, hand me a spade! I have a lot of catching up to do."

Mrs. Moss said, "This is so kind of you all. Where will you start digging?

"The spring house is gone. And you'll all get dirty digging near Egg Rock."

Dave said, "That's OK, Mrs. Moss. We can start digging on the south side of the rock, like the quilt shows.

"You can help me figure out where the spring house used to be ... and put sticks into the ground to mark the corners. The rainbow ends where the door used to be."

The others began to dig, like dogs after a bone. The dirt flew up.

Before long they were all covered with mud and dust.

Sammy said, "I'm getting used to being dirty. I like it!"

Bill said, "Then don't take a shower when you get home. I'll just plant seeds on you and enter you in a garden show."

Sammy stuck out his tongue.

The ground got damp as they dug deeper. They were nearing the water level of the pond.

111

Just then Bill's spade slid off something hard in the wet dirt.

He grabbed a small hand shovel and said, "Wait a minute. It's probably only a rock, but let me look."

He got to his knees. He leaned into the hole.

He began to dig all around the hard thing.

He rubbed the dirt off of it a little.

He said, "Holy cats! This is no rock. It's a jar!"

Dave and Mrs. Moss hurried over.

There was a muddy brown pottery jar, about the size of a loaf of bread.

Sammy yelled, "Yipee!"

Bill lifted it out of the hole.

He emptied it out into the biggest spade. Out came muddy water.

And out came dozens of metal spoons. They were black all over, but Mrs. Moss knew what they were right away.

She exclaimed, "My great-great-grandma's silver spoons! So that's what happened to them! Why, I haven't thought of them in years.

"My mother brought them all the way from Ohio when she and my father came here to farm.

"I wonder what happened to the beautiful silver tea pot that came with these?"

Sammy grabbed a spade.

He ran toward the place where the

spring house had once been.

He shouted, "Let me at that other place on the map, the spring-house door!"

Everyone hurried after him.

After twenty minutes of digging they found some pieces of a small, rotten trunk. And a lot more!

Half an hour later, they were driving back to their house in the woods. They found Mr. Whip sitting in his car in front of it.

He jumped out and followed them up the driveway.

He called, "We did it! I signed the papers. The Wetlands will belong to Bluff Lake ... forever!"

Then he took a good look at them.

He said, "Good grief! What happened to you!"

In front of him stood the Woodland family, with Mrs. Moss and Chief Hemster.

Their hands were all black with soot and mud.

Their shoes were muddy.

Their faces were muddy.

But all of them were smiling.

They took off their shoes outside the door.

They put newspaper on the dining-room chairs, to sit on later.

115

They washed their hands and faces in the kitchen. The sink looked like a mud hole when they were done.

Soon Kathy and Sammy were mixing something in a bowl.

At last they all went into the dining room to rest and talk.

Mrs. Moss showed the silver spoons to Mr. Whip.

And they showed him the things they had found in the second hole ... and a teapot as black as mud, a sugar bowl, and a cream pitcher.

Mrs. Moss said, "This will be beautiful silver when we clean it. I wish everyone could see all these wonderful things."

Dave said, "Hey! Why can't they?

What's to stop us from building a new log farmhouse on the Wetlands?"

Bill said, "We could use the old fireplace stones for a new fireplace!"

Chief Hemster said, "We could hang the quilt from the farmhouse wall."

Kathy said, "We could set up the whole inside the way Mrs. Moss remembers it. And display the silver things."

Mrs. Moss said, "We can use all the old kitchen tools I saved from my farm days."

Sammy said, "And every day you could go to it, and show people how to use them, like a grandmother would.

"I never knew my grandmother, so you can be mine. And the whole town's!"

Mrs. Moss said, "You mean great-grandmother. I'd love it, Sammy." She gave him a hug.

Mrs. Tandy said, "We could plant an old-time garden next to the cabin."

Sammy said, "We could—HEY! OUR OATMEAL COOKIES! I SMELL THEM! THEY'RE DONE!"

He jumped out of his seat.

Bill, Kathy, Dave, and Mrs. Tandy raced after him. So did Mop.

They were in the kitchen for several minutes.

There was a lot of whispering out there.

Finally they came back with popcorn, a big plate of cookies, and a home-made chocolate cake.

Mrs. Tandy said, "Mr. Whip, you get to cut the cake. We all washed our hands, but you look the cleanest to me. Besides, you're the guest of honor at this birthday party."

Mr. Whip said, "Who was born today,

Mrs. Tandy?"

Sammy said, "Not WHO was born! WHAT was born! Today the Wetlands Farm Park was born! So cut the cake!"

And the muddy Woodlanders and their friends sat down for the party.